ZACH RILEY

QUARTERBACK CRISIS

Text by Paul Hoblin
Illustrated by Andrés Martínez Ricci

Published by ABDO Publishing Company, PO Box 398166,
Minneapolis, MN 55439. Copyright © 2013 by Abdo Consulting Group,
Inc. International copyrights reserved in all countries. No part of this
book may be reproduced in any form without written permission
from the publisher. SportsZone™ is a trademark and logo of ABDO
Publishing Company.

Printed in the United States of America,
North Mankato, Minnesota
052012
092012

Text by: Paul Hoblin
Illustrator: Andrés Martínez Ricci

Editor: Chrös McDougall
Series Designer: Craig Hinton

Library of Congress Cataloging-in-Publication Data
Riley, Zach.
  Quarterback crisis / by Zach Riley ; illustrated by Andres Ricci ; text
by Paul Hoblin.
      p. cm. -- (Zach Riley)
  Summary: Sixth-grader Drew Howard is frustrated and planning to
quit the team, because now that he is playing organized football he
can not seem to throw a good pass--but a new boy, Tyler Wade, forces
him to realize that quitting is not the answer to his problems.
  ISBN 978-1-61783-534-6
  1. Football stories. 2. Quarterbacks (Football)--Juvenile fiction. 3.
Teamwork (Sports)--Juvenile fiction. 4. Frustration--Juvenile fiction.
[1. Football--Fiction. 2. Quarterbacks (Football)--Fiction. 3. Teamwork
(Sports)--Fiction. 4. Frustration--Fiction. 5. Emotions--Fiction.] I.
Martínez Ricci, Andrés, ill. II. Hoblin, Paul. III. Title.
  PZ7.R4572Qud 2012
  813.6--dc23
                                        2012007902

TABLE OF CONTENTS

ONE

The Red Rock Raiders were losing by a touchdown to the Wolverines. They only had time for one more play. But Drew "The Dart" Howard wasn't worried.

No way.

Drew was the Raiders' quarterback. He'd *always* been the quarterback. He was in fifth grade, as were all of his teammates. This was the first year any of them had played organized tackle football. In fact, this was their first game of the season.

But most of these guys had been playing touch football together for years. Drew knew them, and they knew him. They all had complete confidence in one another.

Most importantly, they had complete confidence in Drew's right arm. That's how he got his nickname. His passes spiraled through the air with serious speed and were almost always on target.

So when Drew told them in the huddle not to sweat it, they believed him. When he said they were going to score a touchdown, teammate Eddie Nelson said, "You're the man, Dart!"

When Drew said, "Ready?" the rest of the team yelled, "Break!" and ran to their positions on the field.

Which brought them all to this exact moment: down a touchdown, one last play to score.

The end zone was still 15 yards away. *No problem*, thought Drew the Dart. There was even a nice warm breeze at his back, ready to carry his pass into the end zone.

He got under center and said, "Ready . . . set . . . hut!"

He took the snap, took a few steps back, and turned to see whether Tyler Wade, his receiver, was open. Tyler was new at school. He was the only kid Drew hadn't been playing with for as long as he could remember. And the new kid had wheels.

Sure enough. There Tyler was now, his long legs moving so fast he was practically a blur.

A wide-open blur.

Out of the corner of his eye, Drew saw a Wolverines player break through the offensive line. In a second or two, the kid would be close enough to lower his shoulder and crash into him.

But Drew the Dart wasn't worried about that, either. A second or two was plenty of time to get the pass off.

He reached his arm back and heaved the ball just as the player collided into him. Even as Drew fell to the ground, he watched his pass move through the air.

To his surprise, it wasn't spiraling through the air. It was wobbling. It was flipping. It was doing everything but spiraling.

Drew lay on his back and watched his pass tumble out of the air, 10 yards shorter than he'd intended.

Drew the Dart hadn't thrown a dart at all.

TWO

Drew the Dart had thrown a duck.

That's what his dad called passes that wobbled in the air. Sometimes, when his dad was watching games on TV, he actually *quacked*.

"Quack, quack!" he'd yell when a college or pro quarterback made a particularly ugly pass.

Drew always laughed when his dad did this. But right now, as he lay on the ground and thought about his own pass wobbling through the air, it didn't seem so funny.

The game had been over for a while now. His team had lost. And his ugly pass was the reason they'd lost.

Finally, he sat up and watched the Wolverines celebrate their victory. They high-fived. They slapped each other's shoulder pads. Many of them had their helmets off. Drew watched their mouths open and close. They were congratulating each other—that must be what they were doing. But for some reason Drew couldn't hear their shouts of joy.

He turned his head to his own team. Most of their helmets were still on and pointed to the ground. They stood together, to the side of the field, a blob of misery. Coach Mallory stood next to them. His head was hanging, too.

If any of them were saying anything, Drew couldn't hear what it was.

Finally, he looked at his dad, Andy. He was a middle school gym teacher. Andy was able to leave work in time to attend most of Drew's games. Usually Drew could hear him cheering like crazy next to the field. But he definitely wasn't cheering right now. He stood on the opposite sideline with his lips sealed.

Even if his dad was cheering for him, though, Drew wouldn't be able to hear him. Not at the moment. To Drew, everything they said just sounded like quacking.

From the Wolverines: *Quack!*

From his team: *Quack!*

From his father: *Quack!*

"Shake it off, Dart!" someone shouted.

But whoever said it might as well have said *Duck.*

//////

"Hey, Dart!" the voice said. "Yo, Dart!"

Still sitting on the field, Drew looked for the source of the voice.

"You okay, Dart?"

It was Tyler. Tyler Wade, the new kid. The kid who had been wide open in the end zone. In fact, that's where he still stood: wide open in the corner of the end zone, more than 15 yards from where Drew sat.

"You all right, Dart?"

It was weird hearing his nickname come out of Tyler's mouth—Drew hardly knew the kid. Was Tyler mocking him? Was that why he was trying to get his attention? It could only be for one reason, Drew figured. To tell his quarterback, *Here I am, Dart—right where you were supposed to throw the ball. You call that pass a dart, Dart?*

"Hey!" Tyler yelled. "Wanna try that throw again?"

Now Drew was getting confused. Tyler didn't seem to be yelling out of anger. It was hard to tell, though, because Tyler was so far away.

"What?" Drew asked.

"Wanna make that throw again, so you know you can do it?"

It was only now that Drew noticed Tyler was holding the football. It must have rolled to him after it landed 10 yards short.

"Here!" Tyler said. He brought his arm back and chucked the ball toward Drew. The ball cut through the air in a perfect spiral. If Drew hadn't put his hands up to catch it, it would have hit him in the chest.

Bull's eye.

《《《《《

Drew sat down on the field and stared at Tyler. Tyler stood in the back of the end zone waiting for him to stand up and throw it back.

But Drew wasn't going to throw it back. Not after the wobbly pass he'd thrown earlier. Certainly not after the perfect throw Tyler had just made. What if Drew threw another duck? What would everyone think of him? Why would they even want him as their quarterback when there was another kid on the team who could throw like Tyler just did?

Drew was still looking at Tyler, but he was aware of everyone else: the players, the coaches, the parents. They were all looking at *him*.

"What's the point?" Drew hollered to Tyler. "The game's over."

He set the ball on the ground, stood up, and walked off the field.

THREE

"There you go," Drew's dad said. "See? All it takes is some getting used to."

The two of them were playing catch in the backyard. They'd been doing this most of Drew's life. But today was different. Currently, Drew was wearing shoulder pads over his T-shirt.

"I feel a little ridiculous, Dad."

"How else are you going to learn to throw with pads on?" Andy said.

Drew's dad thought that was why Drew had thrown a duck in the last game. According to Drew's dad, Drew hadn't yet gotten used to throwing a football while wearing equipment.

After all, Drew had only played touch football until the game against the Wolverines.

To find the root of the problem, his dad said, Drew needed to wear all the gear, one piece of equipment at a time. Right now he had the shoulder pads on. In a pile next to him were his helmet, his football pants, and his cleats. But all he wanted to do was slump down on the couch.

Still, Drew shrugged and threw the football back to his father.

"Now you're getting the hang of it," his dad said. "Now go for the tire."

Drew looked over at the tire swing hanging under a tree branch about 10 yards away. He felt a pit in his stomach. *I'm supposed to hit that?* he thought to himself.

It had been less than a week since Drew's terrible throw. But by now he was used to hearing people tell him what had gone wrong. Everyone seemed to have a theory.

Coach Mallory said that it all started with his feet. "Make sure you're stepping where you want to throw," he advised.

"Flick your wrist, Dart," Eddie Nelson said, even though Eddie couldn't throw a spiral to save his life.

"Lead with your elbow," Drew's mom told him, even though she hadn't been at the game.

Some people thought he'd let go of the ball too early. Others felt he'd released the ball too late.

It got to be confusing, trying to figure out who was right. Still, Drew was willing to listen. Drew the Dart would do anything to make sure he didn't throw any more ducks.

He cocked his right arm back, stepped forward with his left foot and unleashed a pass. It wasn't a spiral. But it wasn't exactly a duck, either. The football didn't quite go through the tire. But it didn't exactly miss it, either.

The football bounced off the tire's side, sending the heavy rubber swinging.

"Nice," his dad said. "You'll be back throwing darts in time for tomorrow's game."

FOUR

But Drew didn't throw darts in tomorrow's game.

His dad was wrong.

Tomorrow's game was now today's game, and Drew threw one duck after another. Whether he was throwing short or medium or long, the result was the same: *QUACK!*

Drew had tried everything he could think of to make his passes spiral. He stepped where he was throwing. He led with his elbow. He flicked his wrist.

At one point he seriously thought about taking off his jersey and playing with his shoulder pads exposed. After all, his jersey was the only piece of equipment he hadn't put on while playing catch with his dad.

None of it worked, though.

By the third quarter the Raiders were down to the Tigers by two touchdowns. The team needed a big play. Coach Mallory called yet another pass play and Drew told the guys in the huddle not to worry.

"Sure, Drew," Eddie Nelson said.

But he didn't sound *not worried*. At least he didn't call me *Duck*, Drew thought. When he said, "Ready?" the rest of the team said, "Break." But they didn't sound *not worried*, either.

Drew yelled, "Hut!" and took the snap. He backed up several steps, looked up, and saw Tyler Wade.

Wide open, as usual.

Drew stepped forward, led with his elbow, flicked his wrist, and tried not to release the ball too early or too late. But the ball came quacking out of his hand and kept quacking until it hit the ground five yards short. "You're not keeping your chin up as you throw, son."

It was an adult's voice, and it didn't come from too far away. Had his coach walked onto the field?

If he had, it would be the first time. Coaches aren't allowed on the field except during timeouts.

"If you keep your chin up," the voice said, "the ball is more likely to spiral for you."

Drew turned to his left and realized it was the referee who was talking to him. That was a new low. How bad do you have to be to have the referee offering tips?

The ref smiled at him underneath his mustache. He appeared to be genuine. But not to Drew.

A smile of pity, he thought.

Then the ref put his whistle to his mouth and blew it to signal the end of the quarter. There was still another quarter to go, but as far as Drew was concerned, the game was over.

FIVE

When the referee blew his whistle again, the game was officially over. Tyler Wade trotted up to Drew.

"Hey, Dart," he called out.

What did he want now?

"A bunch of us are going to shake off the loss by playing some touch football at the park," Tyler said. "You in?"

Drew stared hard at Tyler to see if he was kidding. It didn't look like it. Which meant, among other things, that this was Drew's new low. The new guy had just invited him to play football with guys Drew had been playing with most of his life. Wasn't Drew the one who was supposed to be inviting Tyler?

Drew peered over Tyler's shoulder and saw the others shuffling off the field. They were chatting and laughing. Did they even want him to play?

For some reason—Drew couldn't quite figure out why—something just wasn't right with Tyler. Sure, he seemed nice and all. But Tyler was the best athlete in school. And he had made that perfect throw. How could he *not* want to be the Raiders' quarterback?

"I better not," Drew said finally. "I have a ton of homework."

"Bummer," Tyler said. "Maybe next time."

He turned and headed off the field.

((((((

Drew's line about having too much homework was a lie, of course. Or it might as well have been. He did have homework. But that never would have stopped him from playing before.

Drew was simply too anxious to play. What if he kept throwing more ducks? Would his teammates still trust him?

Or maybe it was a setup. Maybe they wanted him to keep throwing ducks. Then Tyler could take over as quarterback.

Drew wasn't fit to play. But his curiosity was running off the charts.

((((((

Drew hopped off his bike. Pine trees surrounded the park where the team played. As Drew walked his bike through the trees and into the clearing he saw the others' bikes piled up in front of him. Usually he would've set his bike on the pile, but not this time.

I won't be staying very long, he thought. *Might as well hold onto the bike.*

Besides, he liked the covering the trees provided.

Nobody could see him, but he could see all of his teammates.

Drew's eyes shifted back and forth, looking to see who was playing quarterback. After all, he usually played quarterback for both sides. Everybody else went from defense to offense, but he stayed on offense.

Normally Drew wouldn't be too concerned. As far as he knew, none of the others were any good at throwing a football. But then Drew remembered that throw Tyler made to him from 15 yards away. A perfect spiral. A perfect bull's eye.

But it *was* just one throw, right?

So maybe he'd just gotten lucky.

The only way to know for sure was to go see for himself.

"Dang, Wade," he heard someone say. "That one stung."

Drew looked up in time to see Manny Doretti shake his hand and laugh as he ran back to the line of scrimmage. Sure enough, Tyler was playing quarterback. And even through the shadows and the dipping sun it was clear that the throw Tyler made from the end zone was no fluke. The kid had a cannon for an arm.

Tyler threw passes all over the field, and he threw them hard. Too hard. The air was getting darker and darker, and Tyler's throws looked like his legs when he played wide receiver. Like blurs. Footballs banged off guys' chests and bounced off their arms.

But no one seemed to mind one bit.

Instead, they laughed and said things like: "That's going to leave a welt!" and "What are you trying to do, break my fingers?"

Then someone—was it Eddie Nelson?—said, "You should be our quarterback instead of Drew!"

There was a clanging sound. Drew looked down and realized he'd dropped his bike onto the pile of bikes in front of him.

"Dart? Is that you?"

It was Tyler's voice—but Drew didn't answer it.

He picked up his bike and rode through the trees as fast as he could.

SIX

No matter what Drew did, he couldn't shake the comment at the park: *You should be our quarterback* **instead of Drew.**

He thought about it all weekend while his dad quacked at the TV screen. He thought about it all week during practice. He thought about it all day in school and all night as he tried to fall asleep.

*You should be our quarterback **instead of Drew.***

They want Tyler to play quarterback instead of me, Drew thought.

He was surprised how much the comment hurt. Drew knew he was struggling to throw the football. But to hear his teammates say it out loud made it worse. Before, there was always the chance that Drew was overreacting.

That's why none of Drew's teammates asked him to play, he figured. Before, there was always the possibility that he was mistaken. Maybe they'd just forgotten to invite him. At least that's what he'd been able to tell himself.

But now it was clear that there had been no mistake. It was official. The evidence was in.

You should play quarterback instead of Drew.

That's what they'd said. He'd heard it loud and clear.

Okay, *they* didn't say it. *He* said it—whoever *he* was. (The more he thought about it, the more certain he was that it had been Eddie Nelson.) Still, *they* didn't tell him they disagreed with the comment. Not right then, when the comment was made, and not all week, either.

You should play quarterback instead of Drew.

It stung even worse than the scratches on his arms he'd gotten as he raced home through all those pine trees.

It stung even worse than a Tyler Wade pass. Which, according to his teammates, stung pretty bad.

You should play quarterback instead of Drew.

Still, the one thing Drew couldn't figure out is why Tyler had asked him to play. Did he really want Drew there? Maybe Tyler was trying to rub it in that he was better than Drew? Or maybe, just maybe, Drew was overreacting?

You should play quarterback instead of Drew.

The remark still hurt a week later, during their football game. It hurt so badly, in fact, that Drew began hoping someone from the other team, the Spartans, would crash into him at full speed. His dad told him one time that a famous announcer—John Madden?—liked to say "you can only have one owie." In other words, you only felt the pain of one injury at a time.

Drew didn't know if this was true, but he hoped it was. He hoped he got steamrolled by the entire Spartans' defense. Anything to take his mind off that comment in the park.

The Raiders were losing big-time once again as Drew got under center in the fourth quarter. He looked over his offensive line and picked out the biggest kid on the other team.

Come on, buddy, he thought, *crush me to a pulp*.

Then he said, "Ready . . . set . . . hut!" and took the snap.

Drew waited for the big kid or any other Spartan to break through the line and charge at him, but no one did. Drew's offensive line was blocking so well that he could probably stand there

all day without anyone laying so much as a pinky on him.

So he reached back and flung the ball into the air. He wasn't throwing to anyone in particular, and the ball didn't go to anyone in particular. It wobbled in the air and bounced on the ground.

As the Raiders huddled up again, Drew heard Coach Mallory call a time out. He watched his coach walk toward them. The man was a fidgeter. He constantly tugged at the brim of his cap. When he got to the huddle he adjusted and readjusted his pants before speaking.

Finally he said, "I think we're going to have to make a switch here. Tyler, why don't you play quarterback?"

SEVEN

"How about an ice cream sandwich?" Drew's dad said. "Or one of those ones with the chocolate chips?"

They were at the gas station. Drew didn't say anything. He hadn't said anything since the game ended. But he got out of the car. As they walked across the parking lot, his dad put his arm around Drew's shoulder. "Look, Drew," he said, "getting benched is no fun. But it's no reason to sulk. To be honest, you've been pouting all week."

They stepped onto the curb.

"The thing to do," his dad continued, "is to keep working. Obviously something's wrong with your mechanics when you're throwing—so we'll just have to keep trying to figure out what that is, okay?"

Drew didn't say anything. They were inside the gas station now, approaching the freezer.

"The worst thing you can do is quit working," his dad repeated.

Drew peered over the glass at all the choices: popsicles, ice cream bars, ice cream sandwiches. He slid the door open and reached a scratched-up arm into the freezer for his favorite ice cream snack, the Triple Fudge Peanut Blast.

"Actually," his dad said, "maybe we shouldn't get ice cream. Ice cream is what people get when they feel sorry for themselves. How about a sports drink instead?"

Drew took his hand out of the freezer and walked with his dad to the refrigerator with the individual drinks.

"Go ahead and grab a big one," his dad said.

Drew did, pulling the biggest bottle of orange sports drink off the shelf.

At the cash register his dad said, "You're not feeling sorry for yourself, are you?"

Drew shook his head. It was easier to do that than to tell his dad the truth.

To be sure, Drew really liked playing football. All of his friends were on the team. When Drew wasn't throwing ducks they all still joked around a lot. But everything seemed to fall apart as soon as Drew took the snap.

He couldn't stop throwing ducks. And he couldn't help but remember the bullets Tyler was throwing that day in the park.

And then, of course, that line.

You should play quarterback instead of Drew.

If that's what his teammates wanted, Drew had an easy solution.

He was quitting the football team.

EIGHT

Yes, Drew was quitting. And, yes, he felt sorry for himself. But that wasn't why he was quitting.

He was quitting because he was a quarterback who couldn't throw. That's what quarterbacks did. They threw passes. Maybe that wasn't all they did. Sure, they led huddles and they handed the ball off to running backs. But throwing passes was the most important thing. And Drew couldn't do it.

He was a quarterback who couldn't pass . . . so he might as well quit being a quarterback altogether. The only thing left to do was announce that he was quitting. But for some reason he couldn't do that.

He didn't tell his dad on the car ride home, and he hadn't yet told either of his parents at dinner.

The family sat at the kitchen table and ate lemon chicken. For once, none of them talked about football. And for once, Drew didn't feel so down.

They talked about the musical Drew's younger brother Jake was taking part in. They talked about the wild game of dodgeball played in Drew's dad's gym class that day. They even talked about cartoons—and Drew loved cartoons! It was as if the family didn't even notice when the phone began ringing midway through.

As dinner wound down, though, Drew's mind began to go back to football. He began to wonder if his mother knew he'd been benched. Had his dad

found a way to fill her in before dinner? After all, she hadn't said a word about it all night.

And Drew's mom loved football. She loved it almost as much as Drew's dad.

Often, the two spent entire weekends next to each other on the couch, watching one college or pro game after another.

As a lawyer she often worked long days and couldn't make it to Drew's games, so she had to wait until dinner to hear about the game's highlights. Lately, though, all there had been were lowlights.

Drew didn't want to disappoint her. So he decided not to tell anyone that he was quitting. Drew crammed his cheeks full of chicken and got up to clear his plate.

"Where are you going?" his mom asked.

Drew paused, and then replied, "Cartoons."

There, nobody would question that.

If he worked it right, maybe he wouldn't have to tell anyone he'd quit. That's what Drew was thinking as he guided his bike once again through the pine trees and toward the clearing. Eventually, he thought, after he'd missed enough practices and games, they'd all figure it out on their own.

When he made it to the clearing he saw that the rest of the team was once again playing a game of touch football. Eddie Olson had tried calling to invite Drew earlier, but Drew's family was having such a good time at dinner they never picked up.

In fact, Drew didn't even remember the call. He figured he just wasn't wanted anymore. And that made the decision to quit even easier.

Drew walked toward the field. He'd come to say goodbye . . . to the field.

((((((

As Drew walked, he couldn't help but think that he really didn't want to say goodbye. All of his best football memories occurred right here in the park. It hadn't been that long since he last played on this field—only a matter of weeks—but it seemed like forever ago.

That was back when he could throw a spiral. It was back when they all called him Dart.

Nice throw, Dart.

Another bull's eye, Dart.

Now the only guy who called him that was Tyler Wade—his replacement. Honestly, Drew didn't know quite what to make of that kid.

After the game against the Spartans, Coach Mallory told Tyler he was the new quarterback. But Tyler hadn't seemed very excited about it. He'd said, "You sure, Coach?" and "Maybe Dart should get another shot."

Was he trying to be nice?

Drew didn't think so. He might have sounded sincere, but come on. Who would turn down an opportunity to play quarterback?

In a way, Drew wished Tyler was more of a jerk. The nicer Tyler acted, the more humiliated Drew felt. Losing your job to someone who was gunning for it was way better than losing it to someone who didn't even want it.

But Tyler wasn't a jerk. He was just plain good. He had thrown for two touchdowns in practice that day and ran for another.

Drew was still the backup quarterback. He played some wide receiver in practice, and he even made a pretty good catch. But Drew liked playing quarterback. And now he knew that none of his teammates wanted him there.

((((((

Standing at the edge of the clearing, Drew watched Tyler stride with his long left leg and launch the football with his right arm. The ball traveled through the air in a tight spiral and was moving so fast that it appeared in the dark to lodge itself into Eddie Nelson's bicep. It took Eddie a second to realize he had the ball. But when he did, he turned and ran to the end zone on the other end of the clearing. A branch was blocking Drew's view of the play, so he stepped farther into the clearing and saw Eddie jump up and down in celebration.

Drew didn't blame him—it was a great play.

Then he turned to Tyler. The others on Eddie's team had chased after the receiver to celebrate with him, but Tyler was still at this end of the clearing. He stood there with his arms at his sides and his shoulders slumped.

Then he raised his arms and opened his mouth. Drew thought he was finally going to yell out some kind of cheer. But the only sound that came out of Tyler's mouth was small and strange.

Did he just yawn? After a throw like that? That's definitely what it sounded like. Then, without warning, Tyler turned his head and—

"Dart? Is that you?"

Drew only now realized how far onto the field he'd stepped. "Yeah," he replied, because there was no use denying it. Tyler's mouth curled into a grin.

"Glad you made it," Eddie called out. "I tried to invite you earlier, but nobody picked up."

"You wanna play quarterback?" Tyler asked.

Was he kidding?

"No," Drew said with surprising force. "I'm not playing."

"Why not?" Tyler replied. "I think there's enough light for at least a couple more plays."

"Because—I'm quitting the team."

There. He'd said it. Not to his parents, not to his coach, not to the guys he'd been playing with for years—but to Tyler Wade, the new kid.

Then Tyler did something even more surprising.

"In that case," he said, "I'm quitting too."

The sun had dropped so far in just a few minutes that Drew could barely see Tyler's face.

"What?" Drew said.

"If you quit, I'm going to quit, too."

Then Eddie Nelson stepped forward. "Yeah, me too," he said.

By now the others had stepped up alongside Tyler and Eddie.

"Why?" Drew asked, really to all of them but especially to Tyler.

"Because you're our teammate," Tyler countered.

"And our friend," said Eddie.

Drew couldn't figure it out. Didn't everyone want Tyler to be the quarterback? Didn't *Tyler* want to be the quarterback? Thoughts were running through Drew's head when Tyler interrupted him.

"If you're done playing," Tyler said, "I am, too."

NINE

So Drew showed up at the next practice. He was still the backup quarterback. And he still played some wide receiver in practice.

Drew even made a one-handed catch down the left sideline. Eddie even made a joke at Drew's expense. And Eddie only did that with his good friends.

But something just wasn't right. Drew still wasn't handing the ball off to running backs. He still wasn't throwing the ball to receivers.

That was Tyler Wade's job now. And even Drew could see he was really good at it. But what was really weird was that Tyler didn't seem to enjoy it.

Tyler did everything the coach asked. But he showed no intensity while doing it. As the rest of the team yelled and clapped their hands in unison in the huddle, Tyler's hands were limp and barely even made contact with each other. Sometimes he didn't clap at all.

At one point, Drew was pretty sure he saw Tyler yawn again.

When practice had finally ended, Drew started off the field with the rest of the guys, but didn't get far—

"Dart! Hold up a second, would you?"

Drew turned and saw Tyler still standing in the middle of the field. Finally, Tyler actually looked kind of excited.

"Ahh, yeah?" Drew replied.

"Would you be willing to throw me some passes?"

The question's sincerity caught Drew off guard.

"Ahh," Drew hesitated. "I don't know. All I can throw is—"

Tyler cut him off.

"Please?"

The truth was that he did want to throw some passes. For weeks he'd dreaded every pass he had to make. It was one of the reasons quitting seemed like such a good idea. If Drew had stopped playing, he'd never have to throw another duck.

But after watching Tyler throw bullet passes all over the field, Drew was ready to give passing another try.

Drew raised his hand for the ball. Tyler flipped it to him and smiled, but Drew didn't smile back.

"Ten yard button hook," he said. "Hut!"

And like that Tyler was sprinting down the field. He stopped on a dime at 10 yards and turned around. By then Drew's pass was already in the air—and as always it was wobbling. It sailed to the right and over Tyler's head.

Before Drew had a chance to express his frustration, though, Tyler chased after the football, picked it up and tossed it back to Drew.

"Same thing?"

Drew nodded his head. "Hut!"

Once again the throw was a bad one. Once again Tyler retrieved the ball and got ready to run another route.

This happened over and over and over. Each time, Drew tried to correct his throwing motion. Each time, the ball came out of his hand wobbling. Finally, after throwing yet another duck, Drew did the only thing he hadn't tried. He screamed.

"AHHHHHH!"

⦇⦇⦇⦇⦇

Screaming actually made Drew feel a little better. He looked at Tyler, who was catching his breath a few yards away.

"Sorry," Drew said. "It's just that no matter what I do, I can't throw a spiral."

"So don't throw a spiral then."

He said it so casually, like it was the most obvious thing in the world.

"What?"

"I don't care if you throw a spiral," Tyler said. Now that his breathing had slowed down, his voice was louder. "Why do you?"

"Good passes are supposed to spiral."

"No, a good pass is supposed to go to the person you're throwing it to." Tyler flipped the ball to Drew. "I don't need the ball to spiral to me. I just need it to get to me."

Without even waiting for Drew to say "Hut," Tyler took off running. After 10 yards, he planted a foot on the ground and pivoted around.

Drew took Tyler's advice. He threw the ball without thinking about spirals or footwork or flicking his wrist. All he was attempting to do was throw it to his receiver.

And he did.

The pass hit Tyler in the hands.

"Nice throw, Dart," Tyler said.

"Wasn't the prettiest pass in the world," Drew said.

"No, but it was still perfect," Tyler said. He looked at the setting sun. "I better get to dinner." Then he said, "Will you throw to me tomorrow, too?"

"You got it," Drew said.

TEN

The next practice seemed like it would never end. As he stretched and ran and held pads for his teammates, all Drew could think about was getting to throw to Tyler again.

The more he thought about it, the more he agreed with Tyler: that last throw he'd made had been pretty good. It hadn't been a perfect spiral, but it was right on the money. Bull's-eye.

And he was pretty sure he could do it again.

Pretty sure, but not certain. The only way to be completely sure was to throw more passes. Which he definitely wasn't going to be able to do in practice. Once again Tyler was in charge of running the offense—a task that appeared to bore him to tears, literally. Tyler would open his mouth and let out a huge yawn, and when he closed his mouth his eyes would be all watery. The practice probably felt as long to him as it did to Drew.

⫸⫸⫸

It wasn't until Coach Mallory had blown his whistle for the last time and the team had shuffled off the field that Tyler's grin showed up again.

"What sort of routes do you want to run today?" Drew asked him.

"You tell me, Dart. You're in charge now."

They started with the same button hooks they ran yesterday, but quickly moved on to other routes: slants and posts, fly patterns and fades.

With each throw, Drew gained confidence. With each throw, the next throw seemed less risky.

He knew he was going to hit Tyler in the hands because he'd done exactly that seven, eight, nine times in a row.

As for Tyler, he ran route after route and never seemed to need a break. Finally, after Tyler had run a deep post, caught the ball, ran another 20 yards to the end zone and then 50 yards back to the line of scrimmage. Drew had to ask.

"What's your deal, man?"

Tyler was gasping for breath but still smiling. "What . . . do . . . you . . . mean?"

"One second you're dragging yourself across the field, the next you're racing around it. I can't figure it out."

Tyler shrugged. "I'm sick of playing quarterback. I like playing receiver."

How could someone not like being quarterback?

"You've only been playing quarterback for a few days. I bet you'll get used to it."

"I've only been a quarterback on this team for a couple days," Tyler replied. "But that's all I ever got to play before I moved."

Without warning, Tyler sat down on the grass and let his shoulders slump. He could sprint all over the field without getting tired, but just thinking about playing quarterback made him too exhausted to stand. "That's why I moved," he said.

"Really?"

"Well, not quite." He ripped a few blades of grass out of the ground. "My parents bought a house here without even asking me first. I was so ticked I didn't talk to them for two days straight."

He opened his hand and watched the grass blades blow away. For the first time this fall the breeze had a chill to it.

"When we were moving in, my parents said I should go explore the neighborhood. That's when I found the park, and when I first saw you play."

This was news to Drew. "You watched me play?"

Tyler nodded. "I saw you chucking the ball all over the field, and I heard the guys calling you Dart. It was the first time I was excited to be here. No way would anyone make me play quarterback with a guy named Dart on the team."

Drew felt almost guilty. "Except you do have to play quarterback."

Tyler shrugged his shoulders again.

"Hopefully not for too much longer," he said. "Not with you throwing darts again."

ELEVEN

It was hard to throw darts while standing on the sideline.

The only passes Drew had thrown in three weeks were to Tyler, and Coach Mallory didn't seem in a hurry to change that. Drew had been playing well at wide receiver in practice. He even made a couple catches in the Raiders' last game—a win against the Wildcats.

Drew felt good about his passes with Tyler. They were still ducks, but at least now they were flying to the right place. Yet how could he ever regain his quarterback role when Tyler was throwing bullets?

The game was almost over, and it was all tied up. Drew watched from the sideline as Tyler led a drive up to around the 50-yard line. There was only time for one more play.

Drew had good hands, but he wasn't the fastest receiver on the team. The Raiders needed someone fast to break away from the defense on the final play for a touchdown. Drew knew that probably wouldn't be him. So he waited and watched on the sideline as his teammates huddled to go over the play.

He expected the huddle to break up and the guys to run to their positions. But it didn't.

Coach Mallory, standing 10 yards from Drew on the sideline, cupped his mouth with his hands and yelled, "Get a move on, boys!"

But they didn't.

Finally, Coach Mallory hollered, "Time out!" and walked to the huddle, readjusting his pants as he went. Drew watched him talk to the guys in the huddle, shake his head, and tuck the back of his shirt into his pants. There was more talking, more tucking and re-tucking.

Finally the coach's shoulders sagged and he turned toward the sideline.

"Drew," he said. "You're in."

Drew wondered what was going on—if this was real.

"Hop to it, son," his coach said.

He did. When Drew got to the huddle, Coach Mallory adjusted his cap and said, "Tyler says he can get past the defense, and he swears to me that you're the one who can get him the ball."

Drew gulped. But then he looked around the huddle at his teammates. They all looked back at him, nodding in approval. Drew looked over to the bleachers near the Raiders' sideline. He saw his dad standing up, with younger brother Jake on his shoulders.

And next to him was Drew's mom.

"Let's go Drew!" she yelled.

Drew looked back into the huddle. Tyler was grinning through his facemask.

"Just tell me what route to run," he said. "I'll be open."

Drew nodded and called for a fly route. That's when a player runs straight down the field. "Ready?" Drew called out. His teammates responded, "Break!"

As Drew got under center, he looked to his left. Coach Mallory was back on the sideline, adjusting and fidgeting and readjusting. Drew looked to his right. Then he looked to his left. His teammates were ready. So was he.

"Ready . . . set . . . hut!"

Drew took the snap, took several steps back, and saw a blur. It was Tyler streaking down the right sideline. Drew didn't even have to think about it. He reached his right arm back, stepped forward with his left leg and released a dart.

Fifteen yards away, the ball landed in Tyler's arms. He stormed the final 35 yards into the end zone. The Raiders had done it! Drew had done it! Sure, the ball was a little wobbly. But it hit the right spot, and the Raiders had won.

Drew's teammates all ran onto the field to celebrate. Nobody was quacking now. But as Drew listened to all of the cheering voices, he did hear his old friend Eddie Nelson.

"Boy, I'm sure glad Drew is our quarterback again!"

THE END